Raymond Floyd

Goes To

Africa

or

There are no Beans in Africa

by

Mrs Moose

and

Christa

Africa World Press, Inc.

P.O. Box 1892
Trenton, New Jersey 08607

Africa World Press Inc.

P.O. Box 1892
Trenton NJ 08607

First Printing, 1993

Book and Cover Design by Christa

Library of Congress Cataloging - in - Publication Data

Moose, Mrs.
  Raymond Floyd goes to Africa, or There are no bears in Africa /
by Mrs Moose ; art / illustrations by Christa.
    p. cm
  Summary: A tiny bear goes to Africa, where there are no native
bears, and introduces himself to all the animals.
   ISBN 0-86543-375-5. -- ISBN 0-86543-376-3 (pbk.)
   [1. Bears --Fiction. 2. Animals -- Fiction. 3. Africa -- Fiction.]
  I. Christa, ill. II. Title. III. Title: Raymond Floyd goes to
Africa. IV. Title: There are no bears in Africa.
PZ7.M788166Ray 1993
[E]--dc20   93--3555
                                                         CIP
                                                          AC

Printed in Hong Kong by Annboli and Bornmore Limited

To my best friend, Mr. Moose,
and our much loved grandchildren,
Ryan and Amy.

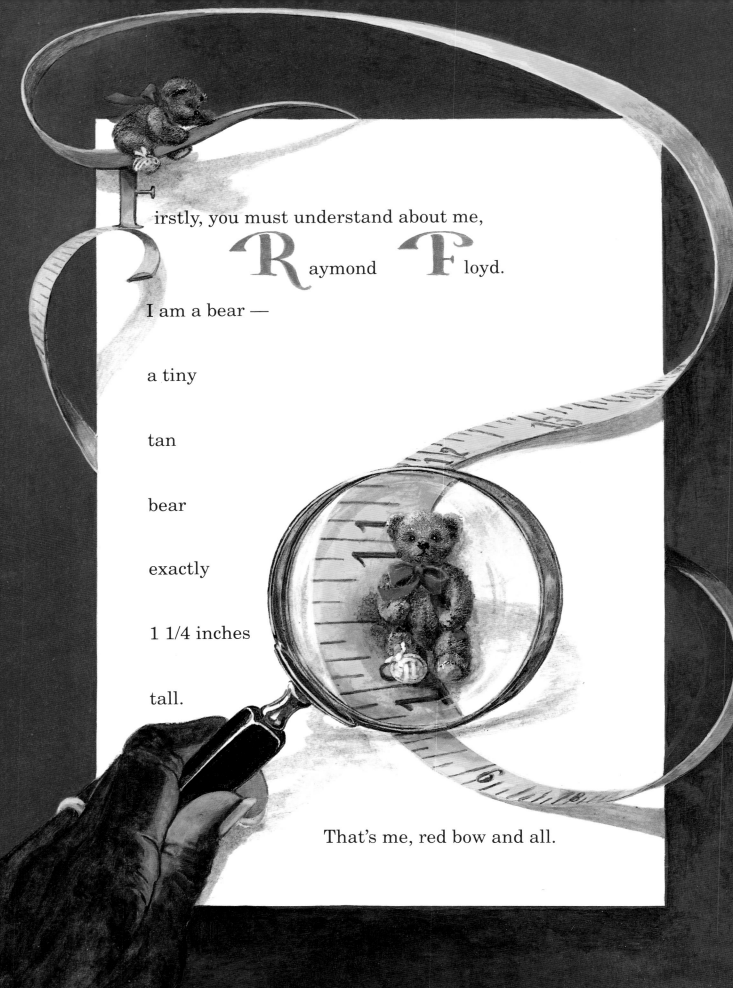

Firstly, you must understand about me,

Raymond Floyd.

I am a bear —

a tiny

tan

bear

exactly

1 1/4 inches

tall.

That's me, red bow and all.

econdly,

there are no bears in Africa.

All those beautiful animals, but no bears at all.
Imagine that!

Lion,
zebra,
giraffe,
antelope,
millipede,
crocodile,
elephant —
animals, animals, animals,

but ...

NO BEARS AT ALL!

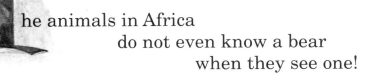

he animals in Africa
do not even know a bear
when they see one!

When I learned this disturbing fact, I decided to go
to Africa to show the animals a bear. ME! I took my
Person with me, because I always travel on her hat.

My person is a bear-maker, and I am one of her
favorite bears. She is called Mrs. Moose, and she
insisted that HER person, Mr. Moose, go along too.
My tour leader, Babette, said that was okay as long
as everyone paid. I DIDN'T!

I rode on Mrs. Moose's
hat — for FREE!
This made
Babette
a little
glum,
but she
survived.
I nearly
did
not.

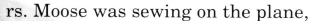

rs. Moose was sewing on the plane,
and I was sitting in
her sewing-box.
She fell asleep and
I fell down between
the seat cushion
and the armrest.

It was
dark and
 hot and

I was terrified. I cut my foot and will have to wear a
bandage for the rest of my life.

Mrs. Moose, Mr. Moose, and the stewardess
(she's the lady who helps you with things when
you are flying) finally took the seat apart and
rescued me.

The man sitting behind us remarked RUDELY
that he did not like bears -- especially tiny
ones.

After many hours of flying, a night's rest in a
hotel room, and some honey for breakfast, we
drove to **Nairobi National Park** in **Kenya,
Africa.**

e rode in a van which after awhile,

softly,

quietly,

gently

came to a stop.

There in the long grass beside the road
were two lady lions, dozing in the sun.

They looked at me;
I looked at them.

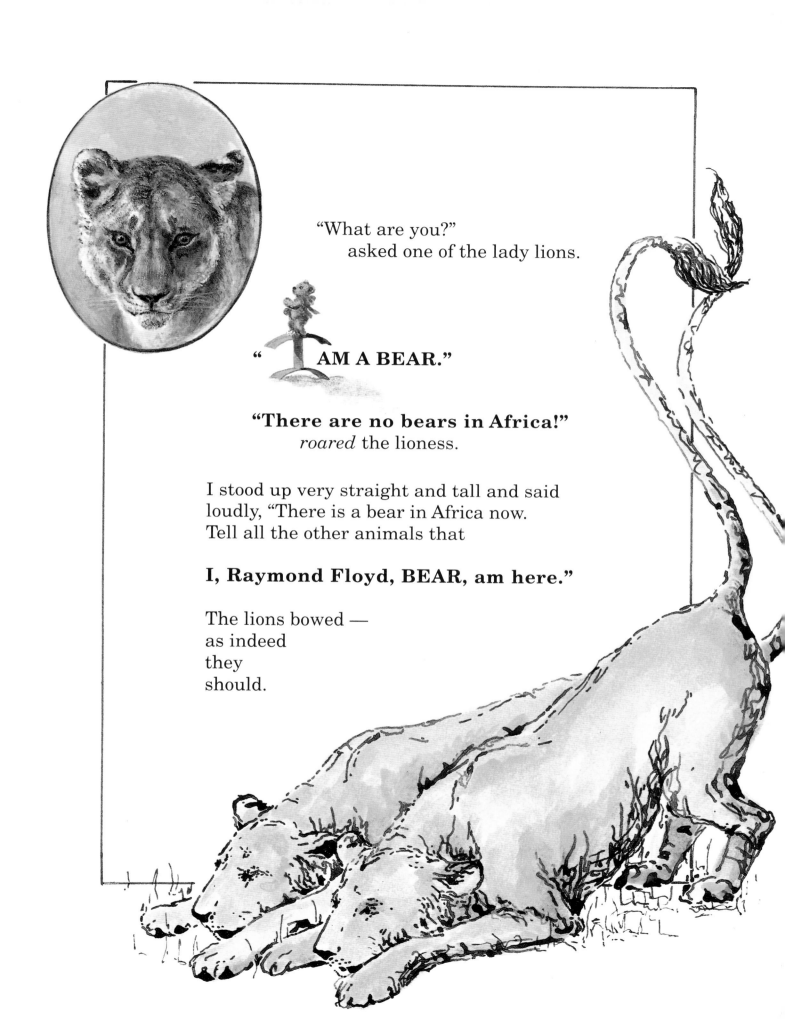

"What are you?"
asked one of the lady lions.

" I AM A BEAR."

"There are no bears in Africa!"
roared the lioness.

I stood up very straight and tall and said
loudly, "There is a bear in Africa now.
Tell all the other animals that

I, Raymond Floyd, BEAR, am here."

The lions bowed —
as indeed
they
should.

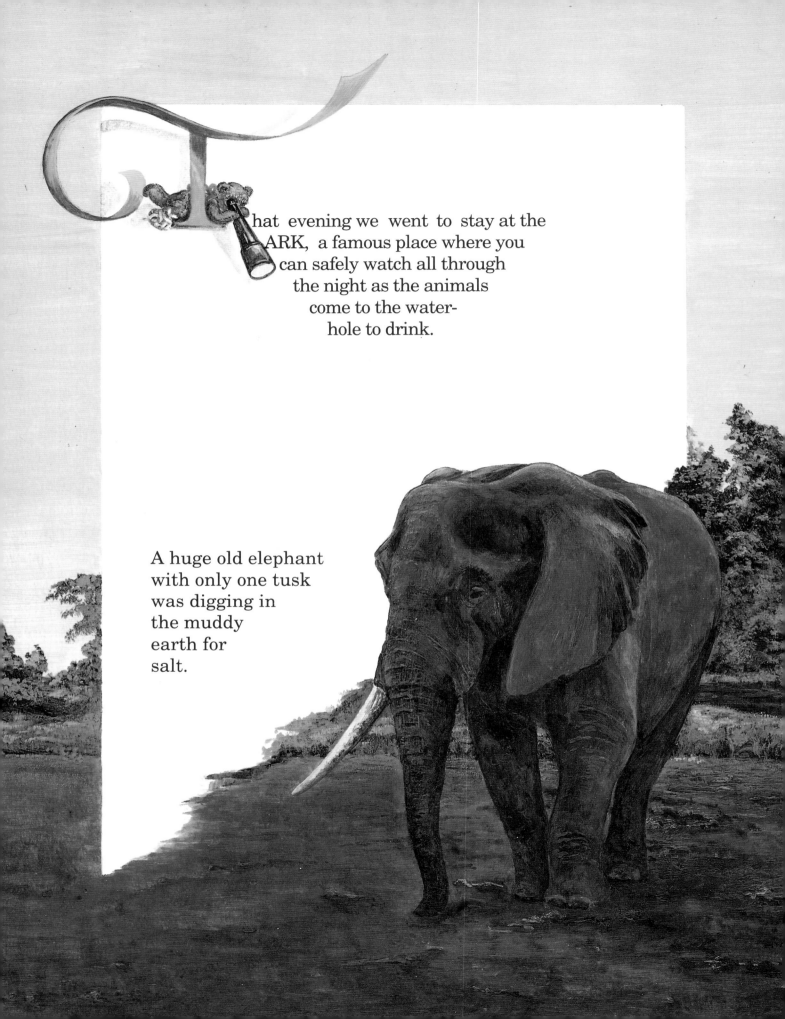

That evening we went to stay at the ARK, a famous place where you can safely watch all through the night as the animals come to the water-hole to drink.

A huge old elephant with only one tusk was digging in the muddy earth for salt.

He looked at me;

I looked at him.
"What are you?"
asked
the elephant.
"I am a BEAR."
**"There are no
bears in
Africa!"**
trumpeted
the elephant.

Said I, "There's a bear in Africa now.
Tell all the other animals that
I, Raymond Floyd, BEAR, am here."

He looked me
in the eye
and politely
bowed his old head.
I was pleased.

In the morning we headed for
Meru National Park.

It was such a l o n g bumpy ride
that my sore foot ached and pained a lot.

But,
it was worth all the bangs
the minute
I saw the
herd of zebra.

uddenly, one of them looked up at me and asked,

"What are you?"

"I AM A BEAR."

"There are no bears in Africa!"

squealed the zebra.

"There is a bear in Africa now," said I.

"Tell all the other animals that....**I,**

> **Raymond Floyd,**
> **BEAR,**
> **am here."**

The zebra nodded their heads
in a mannerly fashion
and raced away.

Properly so.

s I was watching all the zebra gallop off,
the back of my neck began to itch -

just as if someone were staring at me.

I slowly turned around.

There stood a beautiful lady giraffe
with soft dark eyes and long curling
lashes. She looked at me and I
looked at her.

She didn't say a single word!

I knew why: a giraffe has no voice,
so of course she couldn't speak.

(I had learned this
at the Library
when I went
there to
study
about
African
animals
before
my
trip.)

smiled, bowed to the lady, and said,

"I know you are wondering what I am, and why I am here, so I will tell you.

I AM A BEAR.

"You see, when I found out that there are no bears in Africa, I came here so all the animals could see one. ME.

I, Raymond Floyd, BEAR, am here,

so there is a bear in Africa now."
And I bowed again.

The lady giraffe bent her
long neck until her face
was next to mine.
She brushed my cheek
with her long lashes
and nodded her head.

I blushed.

e drove and drove all the next day over roads
that were bumpier and

bumpier

and bumpier.

We even drove right through a shallow river
because heavy rains had washed away the bridge.

We came to a big muddy lake named **Baringo** and
got into a boat to see where the hippopotamus lived.

An enormous hippo raised his head out of the water.

He looked at me;
I looked at him.

"Wʜat are you?" asked the hippo.

"I AM A BEAR."

"There are no bears in Africa!" *grunted* the hippo with disgust.

"There is a bear in Africa now.
Tell all the other animals that I,
Raymond Floyd, BEAR, am here."

"Harumph," said the hippo with a large yawn.

Then he disappeared
under
the water.

I tell you truly — my feelings
were just a tiny bit hurt.

A few minutes later,

our boat
landed on a
lush green island
in the middle of
the muddy
brown lake.

On the way to our tent,
I saw a big black millipede.

He looked at me;

I looked at him.

"What are you?" asked the millipede softly.

"I AM A BEAR."

"There are no bears in Africa!"
whispered the millipede.

"There is a bear in Africa now,"
I said firmly.
"Tell all the other animals that
**I, Raymond Floyd,
BEAR,
am here."**

The millipede riffled all his legs;
that's how a millipede bows.

I liked that.
In fact I felt much better.

After breakfast, we started our
long drive through the beautiful
Rift Valley to **Lake Naivasha**.

We bumped, banged and thumped
rattled,

down the road.

When we finally arrived,
I was tired and grumpy so
Mrs. Moose and I
went to rest
by the pool.

igh   above us in the trees was a
white-tailed Colobus monkey.

She looked at me;

I looked at her.

"What are you?"
          yelled the monkey.

"I AM A BEAR."

"There are no bears in Africa!"
screamed the monkey.

"There's a bear in Africa now," I bellowed.

"Tell all the other animals that
I, Raymond Floyd, BEAR, am here."

The monkey did not bow. She screamed and
screamed and screamed.
And then she SPAT!
I do not like monkeys.
I did not enjoy my visit to
Lake Naivasha.
I like to be
appreciated,   not
                                SPAT AT!

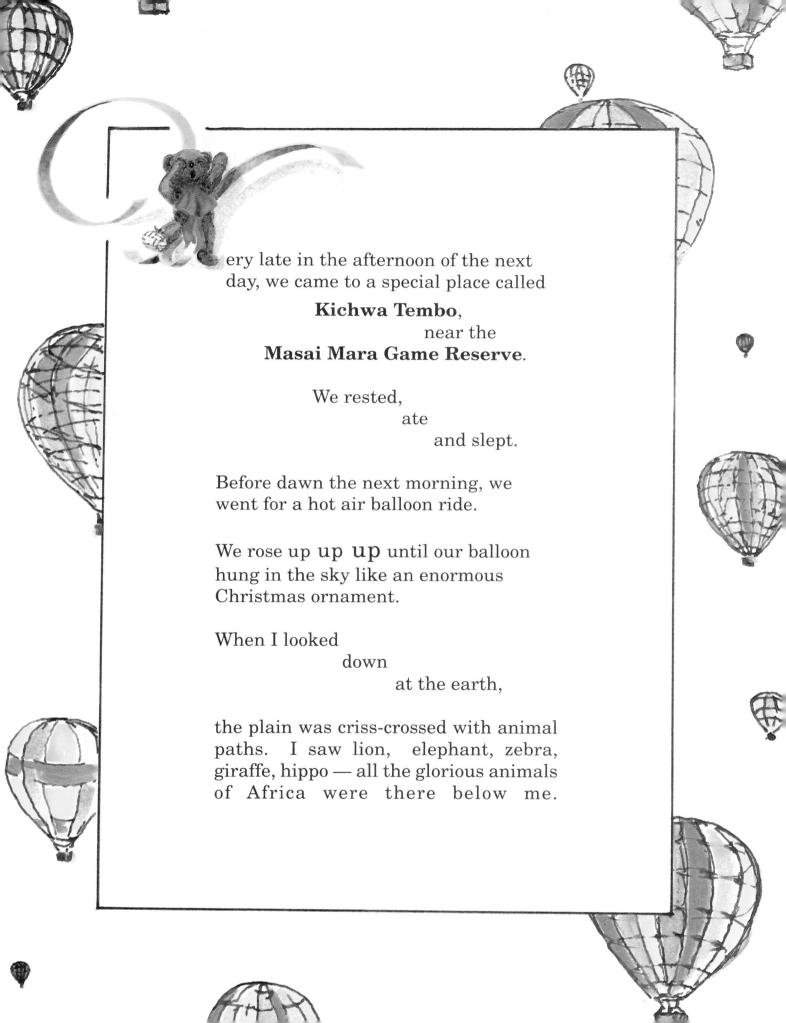

ery late in the afternoon of the next
day, we came to a special place called
Kichwa Tembo,
near the
Masai Mara Game Reserve.

We rested,
 ate
  and slept.

Before dawn the next morning, we
went for a hot air balloon ride.

We rose up up up until our balloon
hung in the sky like an enormous
Christmas ornament.

When I looked
 down
  at the earth,

the plain was criss-crossed with animal
paths. I saw lion, elephant, zebra,
giraffe, hippo — all the glorious animals
of Africa were there below me.

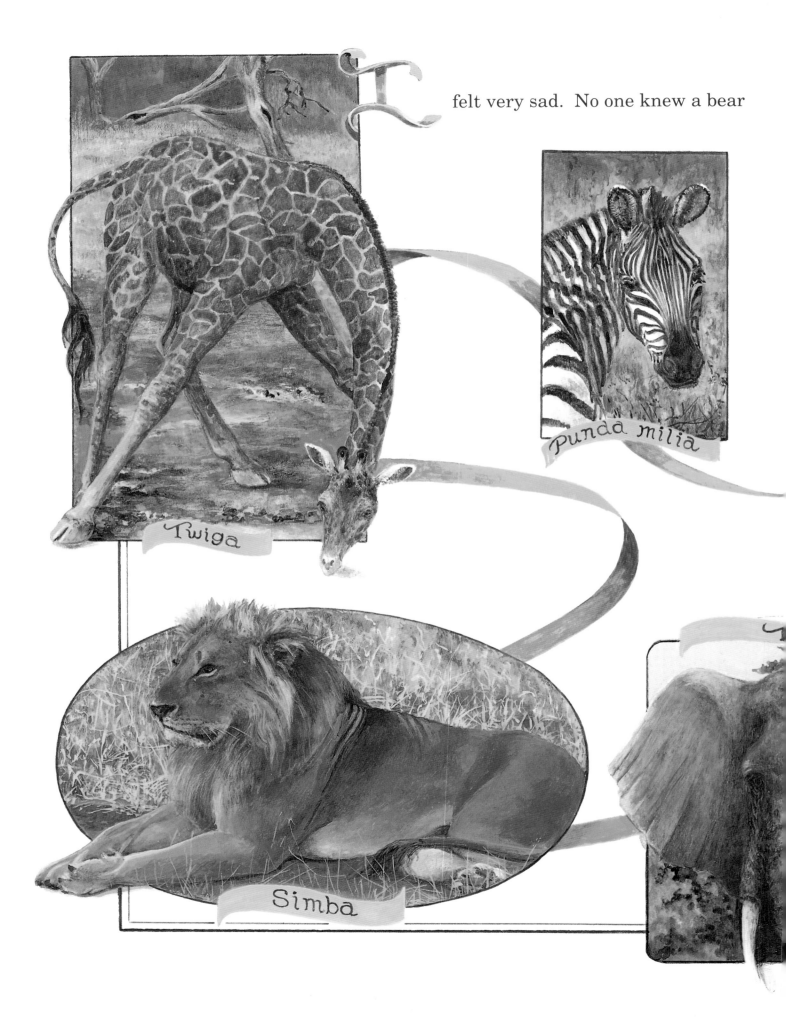

felt very sad. No one knew a bear

Punda milia

Twiga

Simba

when they saw one,

Tumbili

Kiboko

Millipede

and I was lonely.

uddenly all the animals shouted, "

Jambo! Jambo, Raymond Floyd, Jambo!"

Jambo means "Welcome" in Swahili,
     one of the many languages in Africa.

I smiled and bowed and called out,
               "Jambo!"
            as loud as I could.

I was excited and pleased because I had done
what I set out to do.

<u>Now</u> the animals in Africa knew a bear
when they saw one.

               I could go home, and that's
                 one of the very best
                   parts of a trip,
                     isn't it?

Kwaheri !

Good bye !

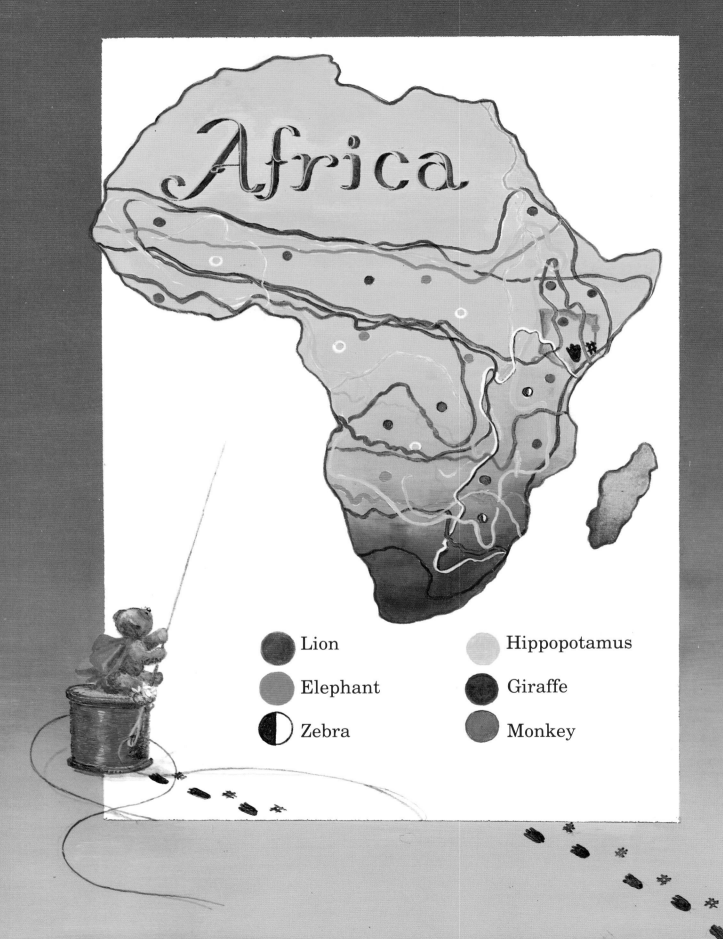

Lion

Hippopotamus

Elephant

Giraffe

Zebra

Monkey

RAYMOND FLOYD'S SWAHILI DICTIONARY

Kichwas	keech wah	head
Tembo	tem bo	elephant
Jambo	jam bo	welcome
Simba	sim bah	lion
Punda milia	pun dah mili ah	zebra
Twiga	twee gah	giraffe
Kiboko	ki bo ko	hippopotamus
Tumbili	tum bi li	monkey
Millipede	mil li pede	millipede
Kikuyu	ki ku yu	tribal name

A P.S. from Mrs. Moose

Children, I want you to know that there really is a tiny tan bear, exactly 1 1/4 inches tall, named Raymond Floyd, and he really <u>did</u> go to Africa on my hat.

One noon, when we, (Raymond Floyd, Mr. Moose and I) were in Africa, I was making a small white teddy bear. One of our Kikuyu drivers, Felix Wambungo, walked by and said, "What are you doing?"

I answered, "I am making a bear."

Felix laughed and said, "There are no bears in Africa."

Smiling, I replied, "There is one now."

So that's how Raymond Floyd and I happened to write this book. He is well and sends all of you his love.

Mrs. Moose

The end

 hank you

My Don, for his love and support, and our grandchildren,
Sean and Christa.
- Christa

Vera Moser, who taught me the art of bear-making.
- Mrs. Moose

Our Father, for His ordered steps.
- Mrs. Moose and Christa